(M) 3.50

CLASSIC STARTS™

Robinson Crusoe

Retold from Daniel Defoe
original by Deanna McFadden

Illustrated by Jamel Akib

Sterling Publishing Co., Inc.
New York

Library of Congress Cataloging-in-Publication Data Available

2 4 6 8 10 9 7 5 3 1

Published by Sterling Publishing Co., Inc. 387 Park Avenue South,
New York, NY 10016

Distributed in Canada by Sterling Publishing
c/o Canadian Manda Group, 165 Dufferin Street Toronto, Ontario,
Canada M6K 3H6
Distributed in Great Britain and Europe by Chris Lloyd at Orca Book
Services, Stanley House, Fleets Lane, Poole BH15 3AJ, England
Distributed in Australia by Capricorn Link (Australia) Pty. Ltd.
P.O. Box 704, Windsor, NSW 2756, Australia

Printed in China

Designed by Renato Stanisic

Sterling ISBN 1-4027-2664-3

For information about custom editions, special sales, premium and
corporate purchases, please contact Sterling Special Sales
Department at 800-805-5489 or specialsales@sterlingpub.com.

Contents

CHAPTER I

A Sailor's Life

My name is Robinson Crusoe. In 1692, I was born in the town of York. I was the youngest of three sons. My eldest brother was a soldier and died in battle against Spain. My second brother simply disappeared. He left one day and never returned. My parents had lost two sons and did not want to lose a third. My father wanted me to stay home and become a lawyer, but I craved grand adventures and faraway lands—I wanted to be a sailor!

One morning, my father called me into his

study. He was a grave man with stern eyes and a sharp mind. He spoke to me for a long time about my dreams. My father had worked hard to give his family a good, safe life. How could I leave it all behind for a life on the high seas?

I could say nothing in my defense. Sailing was hard, scary work. Many men lost their lives. Many boats got lost. Many left home never to return again. This excitement sparked my imagination.

"I know it's dangerous, Father." I said. "But I feel it is my destiny. I'm sorry."

My father started to cry. I felt awful for upsetting him, so I made up my mind to stay at home, for now.

I did my best not to mention the tales I read or the great voyages I heard other men talk about in the streets. I suffered in silence and tried to be a son he could be proud of, but it wasn't easy. My heart ached to smell the ocean from the deck of a great ship. My legs longed to walk the shores of faraway lands. My hands did not want to sit and idle away the days of my youth—I craved adventure. Nothing else would ever make me happy.

A few short weeks passed. I became even more determined to become a sailor. I wanted to run off in the night and board the first ship sailing to foreign seas. But I knew that would make my parents upset. Instead, I tried to talk to my mother.

"My mind is made up, Mother," I said. "All I've ever wanted is to become a sailor. I wish you and Father would just give me your permission to go to sea."

"I'm eighteen now," I continued, "If you make me become a lawyer or force me to learn some other trade, I'll run away. But if you just let me go on one voyage, I'll come back and do exactly as Father asks."

My mother grew angry and refused to ask my father anything. My parents wholeheartedly disapproved. That was the end of the subject.

Mother and Father tried everything to change my mind about leaving. They promised me that I could attend any school I wanted. They told me I could look into any trade that interested me. I refused every offer—my only dream was to go to sea. Nothing else would do.

CHAPTER 2

My First Voyage

About a year later, my father sent me into the town of Hull to run some errands for him. Once there, I ran into John, an old school friend. His father was the captain of a ship sailing to London.

"You are a lucky devil!" I said to him. "All I want to do is become a sailor. But my parents won't let me."

"You're old enough to decide for yourself, Robinson. Why do you care what they think? I'll offer you a spot on my father's boat right now. Why don't you just come with us?"

Yes! I thought. *Here's my chance.*

"Okay, John! Thank you—I'd love to go!"

My parents would be hurt, but I couldn't spend my life trying to make them happy. I was finally going to become a sailor!

We left extremely early in the morning. The sun had barely risen before we set sail. The boat pitched this way and that way in the waves. I became quite seasick. On top of my upset stomach, I was scared to death. The waves rode high. They crashed upon the sides of the boat. Sometimes, they spilled over onto the deck.

I lay on the hammock in my small cabin and felt miserable. I cried and cried. I felt guilty for leaving my mother and father the way I did. They were good, kind parents who only wanted the best for me. I had betrayed them; this was my punishment.

The storm grew worse. The waves rose higher.

I expected every one to swallow us whole. Each time the ship pitched forward over another huge wave, I thought it would never rise again. "If I ever survive," I said to myself that night, "I swear I'll go home to my mother and father and be a good person. I'll be the best son!"

By the next morning, the sea had calmed down. It looked as smooth as glass. My body no longer felt seasick. The sun welcomed me to a bright, enjoyable day. What a difference! I went up on deck for the first time since we left Hull. I saw John looking out over the horizon. He said, "You're feeling better! I can't believe you were that scared of a little capful of wind!"

"A capful!" I snorted. "What a terrible storm!"

John laughed, "That was nothing at all. Just wait until you're out on the open seas. Then you'll see what a storm is!"

I laughed, too. "Well, I made it through

anyway. Serious or not, it was my first storm at sea."

"Come on, Robinson," he said cheerily, "Let's go get some punch!"

What fun I had that night! I lost all my fears in a cup of punch and a rowdy good time. Last night's promise to go home was promptly forgotten. I no longer feared the sea would swallow me up whole. I didn't want to go home—it was a sailor's life for me!

CHAPTER 3

A Rough Storm

On our sixth day at sea we had to anchor at Yarmouth because of bad winds blowing in the wrong direction. There were many other ships waiting there, too.

About a week later, the winds were finally blowing in the right direction. Only they were very strong. John's father, the captain, thought we would be okay to sail, but the men were not as convinced.

All hands were sent to work taking the high sails down from the top masts. The crew worked hard to make sure the cargo and equipment was snug and close on deck. We didn't want anything unnecessary blowing in the wind. The crew made sure the ship would ride as easily upon the seas as possible.

We set off early that morning. By noon, the sea had turned against us. It was a great and terrible storm. I saw terror and amazement in the eyes of the crew. John's father paced in and out of his cabin. I heard him muttering, "We shall all be lost."

I cannot describe my fright. The ship lurched back and forth as it fought waves as high as mountains. A new one crashed against the boat every couple of minutes. Many other ships around us flailed in the rough seas.

I watched as other sailors worked hard to cut down their masts so the wind wouldn't catch them. If the masts were cut down, it would help to stop the waves from carrying the ship under the water. At first, the captain was hesitant to do the same because we were heavily laden with goods. He didn't want us to become unbalanced. Then, the sea got rougher and the storm grew worse.

The captain was soon convinced. "Strike the sails!" he shouted. "Down with the masts! Hurry, boys, or we shall all be lost!" We prayed this would be enough to save us. Many other ships were still having trouble in the storm. One ahead of us had already gone down.

The worst was yet to come. The men huddled next to me in the cabin said they had never seen a storm like it. They prayed. They begged the heavens to save them. But the storm showed no mercy. Even the captain thought the only place we would land was the bottom of the sea.

Just when we thought the situation could grow no worse, one man raced up from below and shouted that our ship had sprung a leak. Four feet of water lay in the hold! All hands were called below deck to pump. I went down and worked very hard.

The water seemed to be winning the battle. The storm slowed a bit, but still the hold filled up with water. The captain knew we would never make it to the next port. He ordered the crew to start firing our cannons to call out for help.

"Wait!" I heard one of the sailors call out. "Here comes a rescue boat!" The waves made it almost impossible for the boat to get to us. We had one chance: we needed to throw a rope to them, so we could stay steady enough to board. We all watched as the first mate carefully tossed the rope out into the open sea. What luck! They caught it! We scrambled to climb aboard.

Each time the little rescue boat reached the crest of a wave, I feared for my life. The waves were so tall! We were so small! The brave men rowed and rowed. They had risked life and limb to help us, and they weren't going to lose us now.

Just fifteen minutes after we were rescued, we watched in horror as our ship tipped over and went under. After what felt like forever, I could finally see the shore. There were men running everywhere waiting for our arrival, trying to see if they could help.

We landed safely! Cries of "hurrah" and "hallelujah" erupted the instant the boat hit the sandy beach. Men all around threw blankets on us so we wouldn't be cold. Our captain heartily thanked the brave men who had rescued us.

Our entire crew walked slowly back to Yarmouth, our spirits defeated because we had lost our boat. The goodness of the people in Yarmouth did much to make up for our loss. The local judge found everyone a warm bed for the night and many of the shopkeepers were kind enough to help us get back to London or Hull.

A part of me wanted to go back to Hull. From there I could travel to York to see my parents. But a larger part of me still craved an adventure. I couldn't make up my mind. Should I stay and find a new ship or should I go home?

On my third day in Yarmouth, I ran into my friend John walking with his father. They both looked shaken and upset.

"Father," John said, "This is Robinson. Remember I told you about how he came along to see what a sailor's life was like. He wants to spend his life at sea."

The captain looked at me carefully. "Robinson, take this as a sign and go home. A life at sea is not for you."

"But, sir, has this one storm also spoiled you?" I asked. "Will you no more go to sea?"

The captain replied. "My life is different. This is my career. It's my duty to go to sea. For you, it was a trial, a test, and a very unlucky one. If you insist on a life at sea, I am afraid of what might happen to you."

He spoke gravely about good luck. He told me I was tempting fate by continuing to follow my dreams. He went so far as to suggest that all the bad luck was indeed my fault!

These were the last words he said to me: "Robinson, you can depend upon one thing. If you ignore the wishes of your father, you will meet both disappointment and disaster."

I shook my head and turned away. I never saw John or his father again after that day. As I walked, I thought carefully about what he said. What if the storm was a sign? What if it meant I should never become a sailor?

"Maybe I should just count my blessings and go home," I said. "What if he's right and I am cursed?" But I couldn't go home such a failure. My father would never be proud of me. So, I swallowed my doubts and rode on to London.

CHAPTER 4

An African Voyage

My luck improved in London. I fell into good company and met Captain Culpeper, who had just returned from Africa. His African voyage had been so successful that he was about to set off on another one. We shared many meals and had a number of great conversations. When Captain Culpeper learned of my desire to see the world, he decided to take me along with him.

Captain Culpeper was an honest and fair man. Not only did he hire me for his voyage, but he also took me under his wing. He helped me buy the items I could trade to make a small profit. While sailing, he also taught me about mathematics, navigation, and many other things seamen need to know. He gave me excellent advice.

The heat in lands so close to the equator gave me a great fever. For much of the time we spent down south, I was sick. After almost a year at sea, we returned to London. Getting back safely wasn't the only good thing that came out of my trip. I found out that I was a good trader. I had made a solid profit from my goods.

Although my health improved when we were back in colder climates, Captain Culpeper had caught the same fever and he wasn't so lucky. He died soon after we got back. I missed him terribly. He was a loyal friend and mentor.

My success as a trader convinced me that I had made the right choice. I ignored the advice of John's father, and tried not to be too sad about

Captain Culpeper. When the first mate offered me a place on a ship about to sail for Africa, I jumped at the chance to go with them. I left most of my newfound fortune with Culpeper's widow for safekeeping and set off on another adventure.

CHAPTER 5

Pirates!

As much as my luck had changed when I arrived in London, the opposite was now true. The second voyage to Africa soon became my worst trip yet. I soon learned that there were far worse things than a capful of wind and a close rescue! As our ship made a course for the Canary Islands, we were surprised by a pirate ship.

They chased us for hours with full sails blazing. When they caught up to us, our only chance was to fight. We prepared our guns for battle. The pirate ship came up on our quarter-deck. We took our chances and fired all of our guns directly into the rogue ship. They returned fire with their large cannons.

All the pirates started firing their guns, too, but not a single shot hit any of our men!

This success was short lived, and within minutes about sixty pirates boarded our ship. They sliced our rigging with their swords, and then attacked our sails. We fought them off for as long as we could with our own rifles and swords (and got them off the deck twice!). Victory was not to be ours, and we surrendered before any lives were lost.

The pirates loaded us onto their ship as prisoners. We sailed to the port of Sallee, on the northern coast of Africa. Most of the men on board were sold up the country as slaves. The pirate captain took a liking to me because I was both young and nimble. He decided to keep me.

In one fell swoop, I went from merchant to

slave. I was extremely unhappy. My father's words echoed in my mind. I was convinced that I would always be unlucky. My selfish desire to leave home would never amount to anything but misery.

I spent long days working in my master's garden. There were also many household chores to do. My heart and body longed to go back to sea, where I would at least have a chance to escape. The master never took me on his fishing trips. Instead, he left me behind to work.

Each day felt longer than the one before, and two years passed slowly. Day and night I dreamt of little else but escaping. Without friends, I had only my own thoughts to keep my company. The work was hard and the sun was hot. Was this how I would spend the rest of my life? Trapped in a foreign country, a slave to a terrible master?

CHAPTER 6

The Chance to Escape

Finally, one day my master took me and another slave, Ishmael, fishing with him. The weather quickly turned against us, and we were soon caught in a great fog. By the time we could see clearly, Ishmael and I had rowed out to sea instead of back home. After some hard work, we rowed safely back to shore.

Two things happened next to get me thinking about how I could escape. First, my master had a carpenter fix up the fishing boat. Now, it was better prepared for a longer voyage.

The new boat is sturdy. I could use it to travel away from Sallee if given the chance! I thought. What luck that our misadventure scared my master.

Later that week, my master planned a fun evening on the boat for some friends. This was the second thing that happened to help along my escape. He ordered me to stock up with loads of supplies. I also had to shine the boat until it sparkled and decorate it for the party.

The next day, just ten minutes before we were supposed to leave, the master came stomping up to the boat. He was angry! It seemed his friends no longer wanted to spend the day at sea. He ordered me to take Ishmael and Xury, another slave, fishing. Even if they weren't going to sea, he still wanted his friends to have fresh fish for the special dinner.

This is my chance! I thought excitedly. *I can escape!* But how? I convinced Ishmael that we shouldn't eat the master's food, so he stocked the boat up with even more provisions.

While he was off packing us a picnic of sorts, I grabbed some other things we would need: candles, a saw, a hammer, some twine, and a hatchet.

Next, I tricked Xury into finding us some gunpowder. I told him we could kill some wild birds for our own supper. He smiled at me and said, "Yes, that's a really good idea!"

A few minutes later, we were prepared. The three of us sailed off into the harbor. We rode out a ways and then dropped our sails to fish. That day, the wind blew in from the north-northeast. I wished for a wind from the south—with it, I could have sailed to Spain. But I didn't despair. Any wind would carry me up and away from my prison on this Earth. I was happy just thinking about escaping to freedom.

It was now or never.

"Ishmael," I said, "The water has gone cold here. I'm not catching anything. Let's sail out a bit farther."

He nodded and raised the sails. We drove another league out to sea. Just before he was going to drop the anchor, I came up behind him and tossed him overboard. Ishmael screamed and yelled, "Let me back on board! What are you doing, Robinson? You're going to get yourself killed!"

I called back, "You are a great swimmer. Head back to shore, Ishmael. I am escaping. There is no way for you to stop me!" He shook his head, accepted his fate, and started to swim.

Xury stood on deck, shivering. He was afraid I would throw him overboard, too.

"Xury, you must swear to help me or else you're following Ishmael into the sea!" Xury couldn't swim that well, so he quickly agreed to my terms.

For the next few hours, I sailed toward the Strait of Gibraltar. Ishmael would have to tell our master which direction we had taken, so I wanted him to think I was headed for the Spanish coast. As soon as dusk fell, I turned the boat around. The new course was due south. It was scary and unknown territory, but it was better than being caught. I never wanted to be a slave again.

CHAPTER 7

The Free Men

We sailed for five days before we stopped. We were well away from Sallee by then and had sailed up a great river. I didn't know exactly where we were, but it didn't matter—I was free. Xury wasn't as excited to be away from the master as I was. He was very scared. The more we traveled up the river, the more he begged me not to go on shore, especially after we heard the loud roar of animals we didn't know. The sun was setting, so I did as Xury asked and didn't venture off the boat that night. We lay down on deck and looked across to see if anything would happen.

Soon it did! Massive beasts came to the water's edge. They made loud and awful noises; horrible sounds my ears had never heard before.

We were both frightened. When one of the beasts swam toward us we both panicked! What if it made it to the ship? What if it climbed on board? What if it sunk the ship? What would we do then? I raced up and grabbed one of our guns and fired into the air to scare the animal. It worked! The beast quickly turned and swam back to shore.

"What shall we do?" Xury asked.

"Well, we need drinking water." I answered. "We don't have any left. Even though we're scared, we must go ashore tomorrow."

The sun rose early the next morning. We rowed slowly toward the mainland, and dropped the anchor. Then, Xury and I jumped in and swam as fast we could to shore. I was afraid natives might steal our boat, so I didn't want to go too far. I had heard awful stories about sailors being stranded with unfriendly people who would steal their boats and all of their goods. These sailors were never heard from again! Xury said he would be the brave man and go find drinking water. I stayed with the boat and kept watch with my binoculars.

A short time later, he ran back. I thought something might be chasing him, so I ran to him to see if I could help. When we reached each other, Xury proudly showed me that he had shot a wild animal. It looked like a hare, but it had different colors and longer legs. This land was one of great surprises, that's for sure!

"Good job, Xury!" I exclaimed.

We ate well that night. We were really happy that we had found water and food without finding either natives or those awful beasts from last night.

My previous voyages to the North African coast made me think we were close to the Canary

Islands, but without instruments, I couldn't be sure of our exact location. Without knowing where we were going, we continued along the shoreline. My hope was to come across an English trading ship that could take us both back to my homeland.

We sailed past lush landscapes filled with interesting animals. A lot of beasts we didn't recognize roamed around, but there were also many we knew, like lions, tigers, and leopards. We stopped every couple of days to find more drinking water. We went so long without seeing people that I was convinced no one even lived in these parts.

CHAPTER 8

The English Ship

Ten more days passed before we came across another human being. The people we met were friendly and helpful. They wore few clothes and we did not speak the same language, but they were extremely generous. They gave us food and water even though we had nothing to trade.

Although the strange people were very kind, we still needed to find an English ship. Our small boat was not prepared for heavy sailing. The only chance we had to survive was being rescued. I didn't tell Xury that I was worried about us making it. I didn't want him to be scared or upset.

We sailed onward. Another week passed. Finally, we came upon some landmarks I recognized. About three leagues off the coast, I could see the Cape Verde Islands. I let out a great whoop!

"What is it Robinson?" Xury asked.

I pointed across the landscape. "Do you see that over there—those islands? That's how we're going to get to England! We're safe. We're saved, Xury! Saved!"

My smiles soon turned to frowns as I truly considered our situation. If we sailed out into the open sea and got caught by the wrong wind, we would be swept away, never to be seen again. I went inside to sit down in my small captain's cabin to consider our options.

"Robinson!" I heard Xury call me from outside. "I see a ship! I see a ship!"

And true enough, there was a ship! It looked Portuguese. I took up the binoculars and watched carefully to see if it was bound for shore. Alas, we were not that lucky. The ship was sailing away from us.

Oh, no! I thought. *I'm not letting them go without at least trying to get their attention.*

"Come on, Xury!" I yelled. "Let's try and catch them." We mustered as much sail as our little boat could manage. We chased the ship as fast as we could, but it soon became clear we would never catch up.

"What do we do now, Robinson?" Xury asked.

"The guns!" I said. "We need to fire the guns and hope they hear us!"

We each ran to our guns and started firing. I hoped and prayed the other ship would hear our distress signal.

The other ship shortened its sails and slowed down! I smiled broadly at Xury and said, "They've heard our shots! They're going to wait for us. Come on, let's go!"

It took us three hours to catch up to them. When we arrived alongside, the men shouted off the deck to us in many different languages. First they tried Portuguese, then Spanish, then French—but we couldn't understand any of them. Finally, a Scottish sailor on board piped up, "Who are you? What has happened?"

I explained I was an English sailor who had been captured by pirates. I told him that I had spent the past few years in captivity as a slave. The sailors were impressed that we managed to escape. They took Xury and me on board, and we were finally rescued!

The ship's captain was very kind. When I offered him all of my worldly goods in exchange for a safe passage to Brazil, he simply smiled and said, "I will take you with us to Brazil—there's no need for payment."

I thanked him for his kindness. The captain was also very nice to Xury and promptly gave him a job as a sailor on the ship. This pleased Xury to no end. And just when I thought he couldn't be any nicer, he offered to buy our smaller boat! I readily accepted his offer. In addition to the boat, he bought quite a few of our other supplies, too.

We had a safe and happy journey to Brazil. I had the money from the kind captain, which meant I wasn't completely penniless in a strange new land. I stayed with one of the captain's friends who owned and operated a large sugar plantation. The business of planting sugar looked interesting to me, so I tried to learn as much as I could.

Plantation life appealed to me. With the money from the kind captain, I purchased a good chunk of land. My plan was to build a sugar plantation just like the one where I had been staying. There was so much opportunity for me in Brazil. But in order to stay, I needed a letter of naturalization, which I found wasn't that hard to get.

CHAPTER 9

Plantation Life

For the next two years, I built up my lands and my crops. They yielded little, mainly food for me and my staff to eat and stay healthy. The promise of success looked excellent, though, and I was pleased with my progress so far.

A young man owned the plantation next to mine. He was Portuguese by birth, but his parents were English. His name was Wells. We became good friends and even better neighbors. Over those two years, our farms developed at pretty much the same speed. We were both well on our way to having successful sugarcane plantations.

Wells and I often took long walks together. We talked about all kinds of things: our farms, our plans for the future, and our pasts. I remember telling him one day that I felt like a man stuck on deserted island there in Brazil. I told him about my father, and about how much I missed him and my mother.

He said that it was natural to miss my parents. He was right. My father would have been happy to see me. I had created a good life. I was happy and safe, and on my way to being wealthy.

We had a good crop the next year as well. I had everything a man could want—a good, working farm, money, friends—but I wasn't satisfied. Deep in my heart I knew these feelings would soon take over common sense. My foolish desire for excitement often got the better of me.

In those days, I spoke about my adventures at sea to anyone who would listen. Each time I told the stories, the tales grew bigger. A group of fellow plantation owners were very interested in my travels. The opportunity for them to become even richer excited them. Soon, we had made plans to outfit a ship for a voyage to Africa.

In my heart, I knew this was a foolish decision. But once it started rolling like a rock down a hill, I was powerless to stop it. I had no need to increase my wealth. I had no need to change my life. I had no need for an adventure. I was my own destroyer. I couldn't resist the offer, just as I refused to listen to my father all those years ago.

The voyage dates were set and the ship was soon ready for the trip. We drew up formal trading plans and I created a will. I left Wells in charge of everything, confident that he would take care of my farm while I was gone.

CHAPTER 10

Another African Voyage

I boarded the ship on September 1, 1659, exactly eight years to the day since I had taken the first fateful voyage from Hull. I tried not to think about it, I didn't want to jinx my trip.

The ship carried 120 tons of supplies, and fourteen men plus my captain, his servant, and me. We didn't have a lot of cargo on board, just what we needed to trade with the Africans.

When we set sail that day, the weather was wonderful. The sun shone brightly. The wind blew in exactly the right direction. We made our way north—meaning to sail for Africa when we reached ten or twelve degrees latitude.

The violent storm hit after we had already been sailing for twelve days. We had to hold tight as it furiously tossed the ship this way and that. We lost three men during that hurricane. One died of pneumonia, and two others were washed right overboard. For two straight weeks the storm raged. We were terrified.

After what felt like an eternity, the weather finally calmed. We were thrown well off course and the captain needed to figure out where we were. I spent hours in the captain's cabin with him trying to decide what to do; we poured over our maps, charts and diagrams.

"Maybe we should make for home," the captain said after much careful thought.

"But we're so far off course," I replied, "it

might be safer to head for the Caribbean Islands. At least there we can refit the ship and maybe find a couple of sailors willing to join our crew."

"That's true." He looked carefully at the papers on his table. "We could reach them in the next few weeks. I think you are right—that's our best plan."

The captain informed the crew we were heading for the Caribbean, and we immediately changed our course. The ship was badly damaged and leaking heavily. Despite these problems, we were confident we could reach Barbados in about two weeks, give or take a day.

CHAPTER 11

Shipwrecked!

Within two days of changing course, a second storm started. The wind blew us far, far west. Once again, we were completely lost at sea.

The strong winds continued well into the next day, and even into the next. Early that morning, I heard one of the men shout "Land ho!"

Almost immediately, we hit a sandbar. The ship rocked violently back and forth. The sea washed over us. I thought for sure we were lost. We ran for the safety of the cabins. We were in serious trouble. We didn't know where we were. We didn't know if the land was inhabited or not. We didn't know whether or not we would survive.

The ship was stuck. It would surely break to pieces if the wind didn't change direction immediately. We looked at one another and prepared for the worst. We were all wet and shivering, our spirits dampened by the events of the past few weeks. Then, there was a change in the wind.

The captain said, "We have a chance now, men! Let's get the smaller boat into the sea and row for shore. It's our only hope!"

Of the two smaller boats on board, only one had survived the first hurricane. It took all of our efforts just to get the boat safely into the sea and all the men on board. The waves crashed around us as we rowed desperately for shore. We were at the mercy of fate. Many of the men prayed.

The only thing that mattered to any of us was getting to shore. Whether it was rocky, whether it was safe, we just didn't care. We rowed hard because our lives depended upon it. Our only chance was to find a bay or a mouth of a river—without that we would be swept out into the storm and lost at sea. We needed to find smooth water so we could make our way to safety.

We had rowed for almost a league and a half before a wave as tall as a mountain rolled toward us. It took the boat quickly, and we were all thrown overboard. The water swallowed us whole in an instant.

It was terrifying. The waves were strong, and even though I was a good swimmer, my arms were no match for the powerful water. I couldn't even break free to gasp for a breath. The water drove me all the way forward onto shore. My lungs filled up with water. I started coughing. But I knew that if I didn't crawl forward, I had no hope of surviving.

Before I could stand up, the waves grabbed me in their clutches and tossed me back into the sea.

The water swirled around me as I struggled not to drown. Almost instantly, I felt my feet touch the bottom. I quickly stood up. I pushed as much air into my lungs as I possibly could before the sea caught me and dragged me back under.

About the third or forth time the sea dragged me under, my chest hit a rock and I lost my breath completely.

This is it, I thought. *I am going to die right here, right now.*

For all of my bad luck, it seems I had one very real talent—survival. The next time the current pushed me forward toward the shore, I gathered all my strength. My feet touched the bottom. I pushed myself up out of the water and I ran as far up the beach as I humanly could. I ran with everything I had left in me. Then, I dropped to my knees. All the salt water in my stomach made me sick for a minute, but I was saved. It was enough. I was alive.

CHAPTER 12

The Island of Despair

As soon as I was able to stand, I looked around. Where were all my shipmates? Were they all lost? Was I the only one to survive? Very soon, the real truth of my situation came to light. All I could find of them was one cap, three hats, and two shoes.

"No!" I howled. "Say it isn't so! I can't be the only one to survive!"

There was little hope for me now. I had no idea of my location. I had no dry clothes, no drinking water and nothing to use to hunt for food. I might not have drowned like the rest of my poor sailors, but my hope for survival was slim. The only thing I had in my pocket was a small knife. What good would one knife do me in a strange place with no shelter and no food?

I screamed at the top of my lungs. My situation was hopeless. Night was falling. I needed to find shelter. There were a number of trees just beyond the beach area. It didn't take me long to find one that looked like it would be a good place to hide for the night. I climbed up and found a comfortable branch. The traumatic situation must have tired me right out because I actually got a little bit of sleep.

The sun shone brightly the next morning. The sea was calm and the storm had stopped. Despite the weather turning favorable, neither my spirits nor my situation was much improved. I climbed down from my perch and made my way back to the beach.

"Oh my goodness!" I exclaimed. The ship was stuck on some rocks about a league away from where I washed up. It wasn't destroyed! If we had only stayed on board, we would have all been saved. But I couldn't think about that now.

Now, I thought, *that's hopeful. All I have to do is figure out how to get to the supplies. I may have a chance at survival yet.*

I waited for the tide to go out. The water was now almost shallow enough for me to walk out to the ship. I pulled off most of my clothes to keep them dry. The water scared me, but I needed to get to the ship. I swallowed my fears and started walking. When the water grew too deep, I swam the rest of the way. There was a rope hanging down off the side of the boat that I used to climb on board.

I took my time and looked around the ship, which had landed almost entirely on one side. The hold was full of water. Half of it was completely wet, while the other remained quite dry. Luckily, the dry half contained a lot of the supplies. I climbed down into the breadroom and quickly ate some biscuits. Once my stomach stopped growling, I started gathering things I knew I would need.

I used whatever spare wood and rope I could find to build a small raft to get the supplies from the ship back to shore. After testing it out a couple of times, it was fit to use for even the heaviest of objects. First, I rescued the dog we had on board. It was a miracle he survived the storm at all!

Many of the sailors' personal items were damaged by water, so I decided to use their chests to store and gather my food. There was bread, rice, cheeses, goat meat, and a little bit of European corn. Rats had spoiled the wheat. I was disappointed by that, but there wasn't anything I could do about it now.

I thought, *I hope the sea stays calm long enough for me to get back.* No more dilly-dallying. I found clothes, a carpenter's chest and some weapons.

That's enough for today, I decided. *It's time to go.* With two broken oars I had found on board, I rowed myself toward the shore. The rocks in front of the beach where I landed yesterday were too dangerous. In order to land my raft safely, I needed to find a small stream or river.

There must be one nearby, I reasoned. So, I rowed out and away from my beach. The sea was still calm, thankfully. The wind blew in my favor, but I knew these sorts of things could change in an instant. The sea rocked the raft back and forth. I used my legs to hold on tightly to my cargo. The dog barked. I couldn't bear to lose a single thing, so I tried to be very, very careful.

I rowed around until I found a river. And then it took a couple of hours to find a good place to land. Once I had pulled all my stuff ashore, I secured the raft so I could use it tomorrow. The next important step was finding somewhere safe to store everything.

The dog jumped off the raft almost immediately. He started exploring and smelling everything in sight. I armed myself with a pistol and some powder. My aim was to find a bit of shelter, something more comfortable than a tree!

I noticed a small hill in the distance, about a mile away. *Maybe I could see better from up there.* With the dog in tow, I started off in that direction.

"Well," I said to him. "You're going to need a name if we're going to be friends. What should I call you?" He barked an answer, and I laughed for the first time in two days. "I know. I'll call you Shippy, because I saved you from the ship."

We walked for a while and it got quite hot. When I got to the top of the hill, I saw that I was on an island. There were no other people around—well, none that I could see, anyway.

There were lots of beautiful birds, but I didn't recognize any particular species.

After surveying the island quickly, I walked back down to the raft. I unpacked and organized my supplies. Much to my surprise, that took me the rest of the day. I ate some more biscuits and then made a kind of hut with the sea chests. I didn't want to get eaten by any animals at night!

CHAPTER 13

A Temporary Shelter

The next day I went right back out to the ship to see what else I could save. It was important to gather every little thing I could. Another storm could hit at any minute and wash the ship away. I didn't want to miss my chance to save something that could make my life better while I was stranded on this island. Off I went again when the tide was low. I dragged my raft behind me as I swam out to the ship, and then tied it to the very same rope I used to climb up.

This time, I decided I could use a second raft,

so I built one using the first as a model. I packed so many things onto these two rafts! I took nails, more guns, some clothes, more food and all the building supplies I could find. I also took the spare sail with me. When the rafts were full, I rowed back down the river to my hiding place.

When I returned, I found a wild cat sitting on one of my chests!

"Shoo!" I yelled. "Go on! Leave it alone!" The cat didn't budge. She just looked at me with her big, pretty eyes as if to say, "You're going to have to do better than that, Mister!"

I threw a piece of biscuit off into the woods. That did the trick! She chased it and ate it in one quick bite. From the looks of things, she hadn't destroyed anything. In fact, no other animal had been there—that was a good sign.

Next up was making a proper tent. First, I cut some poles down from the trees around my new camp. Then, I used the spare sail with some rope I had found on the ship. Once the tent was finished, I brought everything inside that might go bad if it got too wet from the rain or too hot from the sun. Finally, I set up a more comfortable bed with two hammocks I had rescued. Hard work and comfort sent me right off to sleep that night.

For the next two weeks, I carried on like I did those first couple of days. In the morning, after the tide went out, I would swim to the ship towing my rafts. I searched the ship from bow to stern for anything that might be useful. After a good couple of hours of gathering supplies, I would row the rafts back to shore. Some of the more interesting things I discovered on board were a pair of scissors (very useful indeed!) and a razor, so I could shave. I also found a chest with over thirty pounds' worth of

gold—not that I had any use for it. I took it with me anyway, despite not having a place to spend it!

On the last day of those first two weeks, the weather finally turned. It was my very last trip to the ship. I had almost everything I could possibly use, and then some. The wind rose quickly. The goods were heavy as I rowed hard for shore. I knew I only had one chance to make it back before the storm. So for the second time in as many weeks, I rowed to save my life. The choppy water slopped up over the rafts. I didn't even have time to think about what might happen—I rowed and rowed. I had to get back.

My hard work paid off, and I was soon in the comfort of my tent, listening to the rain fall all around me. The wind blew hard against the sail. I could hear the trees swaying, their leaves rustling. The storm must have continued all night, but I didn't hear it. I slept safe and sound in my homemade tent. The next morning I woke up and ran down to the beach. The ship was completely gone!

Well, I thought. *My luck certainly lasted just long enough.* I stood there for a minute looking at the empty space and thought about the ship, the crew, and our captain. I also thought about how different my life was just two weeks ago.

CHAPTER 14

The First Month

Now that I was finished with my daily trips to and from the ship, I needed to build a more permanent shelter. The most important part of my life now was making sure I could be safe from any wild animals or natives.

Would it be better to make a more permanent tent? I wondered. *Or would it be smarter to find a cave to live in?* I sat down on the beach and contemplated both options. *I think I need both a cave for storage and a better tent.*

The beach where I had set up camp was both

too hot and not close enough to drinking water. It was important to be able to see the sea, too, to watch for passing ships.

Shippy and I took a long walk around the island. After about three hours, we came upon a nice grassy plain on the side of a rising hill. It looked perfect! It took me several days to move all of my supplies to my new camp. I didn't want to stay there until I had moved absolutely everything. I left Shippy there most nights to guard my things until there was nothing left down at our first camp.

First, I built a fort around the area where I planned to pitch my tent. I took young trees from the forest and planted them all around a small cave I had found. Then, I built up walls just inside the line of trees. Instead of building a door to get into my wall, I built a ladder—you couldn't be too safe, or at least that's how I felt. But Shippy needed to get in and out, too, so I created a space in the wall for him to come and go as he pleased. I hid it with palm leaves so no one could notice it. When I was done, my fort offered me great protection and peace of mind.

Next, I made a more solid structure to hold up the canvas top. I built my new home so it backed into the cave, which I used for cold storage. The days were busy. As each one went by, I became more hopeful about survival. All of my supplies eventually became well organized; my gunpowder was separated into many different parcels (to keep it safe from lightning!); and my food was safely stored so it wouldn't spoil.

In those first few weeks, I would head out with my dog and a gun to hunt for food each morning. There were lots of wild goats on this island. They became a central part of my diet. All in all, I had done well. Who knew that I could build a fort or hunt for food? Who knew that I had the strength and will to survive? I was lucky. I had food, water, and shelter—the basics were covered.

With life's necessities taken care of, I had more time to think. The hardest part about being on the island was spending so much time alone. My thoughts roamed to my family. It was upsetting to think I would never see them again. I remembered my fellow sailors, the ones who weren't as lucky as I was; the ones who drowned. I spent time just sitting and crying. With the small bit of paper and ink I saved from the boat, I started to keep a diary. On the days where my heart ached with everything I had lost or given up, it helped to write.

It was now somewhere around the end of October. I had been away from Brazil for two months. Right after I landed, I had made a sort of calendar on a big tree by the beach. I had marked each day with a straight line, and then crossed them out one week at a time. We left Brazil on September 1, and I knew we were at sea for thirty days before we hit that sandbar. The tree showed that I had been on the island for one month. So, I created a new calendar starting on September 30, the day I landed on my island. That would become my anniversary. Now I knew one day from the next, Friday from Sunday, Monday from Wednesday, and that also set my mind at rest.

CHAPTER 15

Life on a Deserted Island

Over the next few weeks, I worked hard to improve my camp. It needed to be bigger to store all of my supplies. After many trial runs, I made a table and a chair. This completely surprised me at the time, for I was never much of a carpenter. Time and effort taught me that I could build, carve, or make anything as long as I set my mind to it. The objects I created might have looked rough, but at least they worked—and that was far more important to me.

My days now had a clear routine. I walked out

in the mornings, until about eleven o'clock. These walks were for exercise, but also for hunting. I discovered some wild birds that I could eat, in addition to the goats. It was important for me to use every part of the animals I killed. I used their coats. I ate their meat. I never killed for sport: My powder was too precious, and my conscience would have hated it anyway.

The days were hot. After my long walk in the morning, I usually took a nap. As soon as the sun would start its decline, I would make dinner and start to work on my various different projects. I made candles. I wrote in my diary. I carved bowls for food—anything to pass the time.

On one of my walks, I was happy to discover an ironwood tree in the woods.

"Such a strong wood," I said to myself. "I can use it to make a spade, and even a grindstone to help keep my tools sharp."

Strong wood, indeed! It took me many hours of chopping with my axe to even cut a bit of wood from the tree. But the tools I made were indispensable to me, and all my hard work paid off.

Time flew. In the blink of an eye, I had been on the island for more than three months. Then, the rainy season arrived. The climate had tipped me off that there might be a rainy season, so I had spent much of the previous months trying to build a better covering for my so-called tent. It was fast turning into a proper building, with walls, a door, and a good, solid roof. I carved shingles and then used palm leaves for insulation. It still leaked some nights—that's when I preferred to sleep in my storage cave!

From January to April, I fortified my fence. The stronger it became, the safer I felt. I made a number of other improvements to my house that season, and soon I was as comfortable as can be.

My nights were lit by candles, my house was dry (for the most part), and I had Shippy to keep me company.

I woke up one morning that April completely surprised to find that some of the rotten feed I had thrown away had sprouted. There were great green stalks on my plain. I was pleased to discover that it was barley and rice—they were perfectly healthy crops, too! I remembered dumping the seed all over the place to empty out the bag. I needed it to store my gunpowder. Nature is certainly amazing! I never would have expected the chicken feed to sprout up in my front lawn. But now that it was there, I was very glad it did.

April was certainly full of surprises. But not all of them were good. One day when I was in my cave sorting out my supplies, the ground beneath my feet started to shake. There was a loud crack and rocks started to fall down around me. I was terrified. I ran outside quickly. The ground shook again, and then again. Then, as quickly as it started, it stopped. An earthquake! I had read about them in my youth, but had never experienced one myself.

Well, I thought, *I hope nothing like that ever happens again.* I returned to my house and cleared out the rocks from my storage cave.

Even though the rains slowed down by May, a great storm followed the earthquake. The morning after it finished, I took my usual walk down to the beach. There was something lying on the beach, and it didn't look like the seaweed or the driftwood I usually saw down there.

"What's this?" I said out loud as I walked over to take a closer look. "Why, it's the ship!"

I spent the morning collecting all the pieces and carrying them farther up on shore. Another keg of gunpowder had washed up on shore, too, but it was ruined by the water. Instead of returning home to take my usual nap, I spent the rest of the day trying to put the ship back together. It was hopeless, though. I decided just to save all the pieces. Maybe they would come in handy? It took me almost a month to completely take apart the ship. By mid-June, it was in pieces. I hid everything close to the beach. You just couldn't be too safe.

Life on the island taught me many lessons. Not the first of which happened that June. Because I was spending so much time down by the water taking the ship apart, I was there to see a turtle. I was excited. After months of eating pigeon and goat, turtle would be a nice change. I had a delicious dinner that night.

For days and days afterward, I was deathly ill. I had a fever and terrible stomach cramps. My mind wandered as my body tossed and turned. My nights were haunted by terrible dreams. I cried and cried. I missed my mother and father.

I cursed my choice to go to sea. I cursed leaving my plantation behind. But most of all, I cursed the fates that landed me on this island of despair.

Then, it passed. The illness left me feeling both unsettled and upset. Why did this all happen to me? How would I ever survive? How long would I be here? Would anyone come to my rescue? My body was very weak. I did not regain my strength for many, many weeks.

CHAPTER 16

Island of Discovery

When I started feeling better, I made up my mind to explore the island properly. I wanted to get to know my surroundings. Maybe it would help me to think of the island as a home and not as a place where I was trapped. It was now the dry season. I set out toward the creek where I had first rafted in with the supplies from the ship. Once I got there, I walked along the creek until I grew tired and made my way back. There were lots of plants I didn't know, so I took samples back to camp with me. I also found plants that I did know, like aloe. I was quite proud of my discoveries!

I walked even farther the next day. The thriving green land turned into a thick wooded forest. There were large trees heavy with ripe fruit. There were melons and grapevines! I couldn't believe how bountiful the trees and vines were. I decided to camp out in the grove for the night, so up I went into a good, solid tree and fell asleep.

The morning was bright and clear. I followed the same path and continued north. There I found an opening to a fresh, green, flourishing packet of land. It was magnificent. It looked just like a planted garden. The lime and lemon trees were in bloom, just like the melon trees and the grape vines. There were cocoa and orange trees there, too, but they were bare. I picked as much of the ripe fruit as I could possibly carry.

I walked back toward the first grove I found.

I decided to take some grapes home, too. It took me a very long time to get back to camp. By the time I arrived, Shippy was barking—he was very happy to see me. After all, I had been gone for three days!

Much to my dismay, I discovered that the grapes had gotten crushed on the walk home. The limes and lemons were fine, though. I poured a nice cool drink of water, and then added the fruit. It was truly wonderful.

When I set out the next day, I carried two bags with me so I could gather more fruit. Instead of taking the grapes home, I picked them and hung them on the branches of other trees so they could dry into raisins. Then, I filled up my bags with more fruit and made my way back to camp.

My raisins turned out extremely well and they were quite delicious. I had even built a small shelter in the valley—I called it my summer home!

I had now been on the island for one whole year. The anniversary was an unhappy day for me. I spent most of it thinking about all that had passed. The last sentence I wrote in my journal that year was: "How much longer will I be here?"

CHAPTER 17

Farmer Robinson

My second year on the island started. I had learned a lot about the island over the last twelve months. Instead of four distinct seasons like we had back home in England, the weather here had a very different cycle. There were only two seasons: one rainy and one dry. It would rain for three months and then it would be dry for the same period of time. Knowing this meant I could now start to prepare for the rainy months so I wouldn't have to spend so much time outside.

It was about time I tried to grow some crops.

I had sowed some of the barley and rice that grew in my front yard earlier in the previous year for its seeds. My first attempt to grow anything useful was a complete disaster. Not knowing how the seasons on the island would affect the crops, I planted my first seeds right after a rainy season. Well, that was a mistake! I didn't think about how arid the dry season would actually be! It was a good thing I didn't use all my seeds. I had kept many behind in case I needed to try to plant again.

Now that I knew that my seeds needed wet weather, I waited to plant them until the next rainy season. I also thought that it might not be such a good idea to plant them in my yard. The fruit grew so well in the valley. I decided that soil would be good for my crops.

Success! On my second attempt, the crops grew up healthy and strong. Because there were two rainy seasons per year, I knew I could at least count on two different harvests.

During the rains, I stayed inside. I kept busy trying to make useful objects. First, I tried to make a basket. When I was a boy, I went with my father to watch a basket maker in town. I vaguely knew how to make a basket, but turning these thoughts into actions, well, that was a whole other story.

Before the rains set in, I had peeled some wood from the palm trees that grew near my summer home. These stalks sat near the fire and had been drying for months now. This was the material I wanted to use to make baskets.

The first few I wove looked absolutely terrible. They were all lopsided with uneven weaving. But I didn't care what they looked like and just used them anyway. I made progress and each new basket was better than the one before. They certainly came in handy. I used them to carry seeds, to store my goods, and to move supplies from one place to another.

The rainy season came to an end, and sunny days were back again. My mind started to wander, and I started exploring even more of the island. Within a week of the good weather, Shippy and I were off to our summer house.

My destination was the seashore on the other side of the island. I stood atop a hill and took a good look around to see what the best way to go would be. This hill was quite a bit higher than any ground near either of my homes, and for the first time, I saw that there was land about twenty leagues out to sea.

Where am I? I thought. *What could that land be?* I searched my mind for anything I might recognize, but it was of no use. I had no idea. The closest thing I could think of was that I was on an island in the Spanish part of the Americas. And if that was the case, it was very dangerous. The men that lived in those lands were very unfriendly. I had heard so many scary things about them from other sailors on my travels. They really didn't like strangers and tried to keep everyone off their islands.

I didn't let these chilling thoughts frighten me. I had never seen another person on my island, so I was safe for now. Shippy and I set off on our little adventure. Maybe it was just to hear the sound of my own voice, but I talked and talked to him. I told him all about my life, about my plans, about where I was before I landed on the island with him. He trotted along beside me, happy as could be.

The other side of the island was very beautiful. There were parrots in the trees and lots of interesting animals. I decided to take a parrot home as a pet. I named her Poll.

I spent many nights away from home on that trip. It was a pleasant and enjoyable time, except for the few days Shippy and I spent lost in a vast valley. How glorious home is when you've been away! My eyes feasted on everything! Even my odd-looking baskets put a smile on my face.

"Ah, Shippy," I said as I collapsed into the comfort of my hammock, "Home sweet home."

This was an important moment. As I lay there, sipping my fruity water, and rocking back and forth in my hammock, I stopped feeling sorry for myself. Yes, I was stuck on this island. Yes, I was all alone. And it's true, this was a hard life, but it was also an interesting one. I was thankful to be alive and to have survived the shipwreck.

CHAPTER 18

Life Goes On

In my third year on the island, everyday life really started to take shape. I was busy hunting and cooking in the mornings, just as I had every morning for two years now. I spent afternoons working on projects, like building shelves and improving both of my homes.

Some days I would head out to my valley and check on my crops. They were doing quite well, despite all the attention they received from local birds and hares! To solve the first problem, I hung feathers all around to scare the birds off. To solve the second problem, I built a fence around my crops so the wild hares couldn't get in. Both solutions worked and soon the crops were undisturbed by the local wildlife.

The harvest that year was quite small, so I decided just to replant the seeds I sowed. One of the comforts of my old life that I strongly desired to have was bread. I needed to make sure I had enough barley and rice to make that dream a reality.

When the rains started, like usual, I stayed inside as much as possible. I spent a good few weeks trying to teach Poll to speak, and she eventually learned to say a few words and phrases.

That season was also the start of my pottery making. There was a good amount of natural clay on the island. I made many attempts to bake the objects I shaped in the fire. But each time they would emerge broken.

What am I doing wrong? I wondered.

I experimented with different types of heat. Soon, I learned that they didn't break if I set them on the embers, instead of directly into the fire. Like my baskets, the bowls were far from perfect. I made a lot of pots for cooking and started to enjoy a variety of different dinners, like stew and broth! What a change from my usual meals of fire-roasted meat.

That year, my second harvest was also successful. I now had enough seeds in storage that I felt comfortable trying to make bread. The biscuits I had saved from the ship had long run out and I craved something like them. First, I carved a large bowl from the piece of ironwood I had chopped off almost two whole years ago. Next, I put some of my corn into the bowl and tried to grind it into meal. After that, I strained the meal through some old clothes, hoping to separate out the husks.

Now I had flour. Having no yeast to make it

rise or any butter to add flavor and grease to bake with, I simply mixed the flour with water and hoped for the best. Well, these loaves were little better than flatbread, but they were delicious nonetheless.

The harvests continued to be successful. I didn't want to destroy any seeds, so I started only planting once a year. I knew how much seed I needed, how much flour I could make and actually use—I didn't want to anything to go to waste.

CHAPTER 19

A Boat

The September that started my fourth year on the island, I thought long and hard about moving to the other side of the island. There was little doubt that it was far more beautiful then where I had decided to settle. I also was inspired by the fact that I could see land from there. It made me want to escape. I remembered young Xury and our boat and I wished I had that very boat with me on the island. How far I could have gone!

In spite of this longing to return to civilization, I was also afraid to leave the island. What if I ended up somewhere even worse? Plus, I had now been here for quite some time and I had never seen another human being. For that matter, I hadn't seen much of anything.

"You know from experience, Robinson," I said to myself, "That the worst always seems to happen when you venture away from home." No, I wouldn't move my camp. It was safe and comfortable, and I needed to stay put for now.

That didn't mean I stopped thinking about getting off the island. I desperately wanted a boat. The parts from our ship were still hidden down by the beach. Maybe there was some way I could repair it after all?

Well, that was a foolish thought. After weeks of hard work, I was forced to come to the same conclusion—there was no fixing that boat!

Still, I had to have a boat. My mind was made up. I said out loud: "I'll just have to build one then!"

Again, what a foolish plan! I didn't think it through before I started. I spent weeks in the woods chopping down the perfect tree. Once it fell, I spent nearly four months shaping the bottom and digging out the inside. When that was all done, I had a mid-sized canoe. There was just one problem. How would I get the boat to water? Right now it sat in the middle of the forest!

I pushed. I pulled. I tugged. I kicked and screamed. The boat simply would not budge. And there was no way I could drag it all the way through the forest and the valley, then on to the beach. What on Earth was I thinking?

My struggle with the canoe ended up in nothing but frustration. This boat was forever stuck on land. "It's funny if you think about it," I said to Shippy. "On the beach, I've got pieces of a boat that won't float. In the forest, I've got a canoe that would float, but I can't get it to water!"

And so, I celebrated my four-year anniversary on the island with two boats, neither of which would help me to escape from my island!

Despite the mishaps with the boats, there was enough food to eat and plenty of water to drink. My house was safe and dry (most of the time!). There were things that I missed from home, like carrots and peas, but I was healthy and that's all that really mattered. All in all, year four was good.

The rainy season started, and it came time for me to try and fix my clothes. I had rescued as many of the sailors' clothes as I could from the ship all those years ago. The most important items I saved were the shirts. In total, I had about two dozen of them. The shirts were made out of linen. They were light and quite comfortable, but they were also getting worn out. Many of them had turned to rags by now. I tried to wear them one at a time, so they would last as long as possible.

I had also rescued plenty of coats from the ship all those years ago, but the weather on the island was too hot to wear them. Instead, I made them into pants and shorts. If my baskets were awkward, my sewing was even worse! By the time I was finished making my clothes, I looked like quite a sight! My shirts were rags, and I wore pants made out of coats! Soon, I decided just to make my wardrobe from goatskins. It wasn't fashionable, but it was comfortable. In addition to my goatskin clothes, I also made a hat. My skin was very fair, and I tended to burn if I stayed outside for too long. The hat worked well to keep off the sun.

While I was fixing up my wardrobe, I also made an umbrella. It became my most prized possession. Not only did it block the sun, but it also kept me dry during the rainy season.

CHAPTER 20

Another Misadventure

For the next five years, I prospered on my little island. My harvests were successful. I explored the island little-by-little. Shippy and Poll were great pets. There was plenty of food from my fruit trees. The hunting always went well.

Now, it might have been foolish, but I made another boat during this time—and I learned from my mistakes. Instead of choosing a tree from the middle of the forest, I found one closer to the beach. It took me many months to carve out the canoe properly. When I was done, I got it to the water by putting logs underneath and rolling it along. Once I knew for sure it would float, I made a small mast and sail. Now, instead of walking for miles and miles to the other side of the island, I could travel by boat!

My heart still craved adventure, so I set off with enough supplies to last a couple of days. I took some food, wore my hat, and carried my umbrella. The little boat sailed nicely to the other side of the island. I used the small anchor I had saved from the big ship and went on shore to explore. I camped outside for two full days. Once I knew the landscape, I made my way back to my boat. Off I went to sail back home.

Instead of going back the way I came, I decided to go the other way around. Shortly after I started, the currents picked up. The water started to carry me right out to sea. Rowing didn't seem to make a difference. The wind blew hard, and I was transported even farther away. My little island disappeared in the distance.

"Oh no!" I cried out, "Why me? Why again! What can I do? Where am I going?" Shippy noticed my panic. He barked and barked. All I wanted was to get back home. My camp was heaven compared to being shipwrecked or lost at sea. I took the mast and sail down to see if that would help, but the boat was stuck in the current.

The only thing I could do was wait. I threw my hands in the air and watched as the sun made its route across my island. Once it became afternoon, the wind changed. It started to blow north. This gave me a bit of hope. I quickly got the mast and sail back up. Nothing but hard work made the boat move out of the current. I had never sailed so hard in my life. The boat swayed a bit, back and forth, back and forth. Then, I decided to start rowing, too. After almost an hour, the boat finally turned around and headed back toward the island.

By the time I got back to my side of the island, the sun was setting. I needed to make it back to shore before the light disappeared completely. Instead of trying to get back to the river (where I first rafted in my supplies from the boat), I decided to stop in a little cove just before night fell. Thankfully, the water was calm, and I rowed my boat to shore.

Now, it was pitch black. I tied up the boat and decided to camp out for the night. Up a tree I went and tried to go to sleep.

"I miss my hammock," I grumbled to myself as I tried to get comfortable.

The next morning, I rowed the boat very carefully to a small inlet closer to my camp. I was very tired when I got home. Oh precious walls! Oh wonderful fence! I didn't even take off my hat when I went inside—I just climbed right into my hammock and fell asleep. My arms and legs ached. My mind was completely exhausted.

I heard a strange voice call out in my sleep, "Robinson Crusoe!" It said. "Robinson Crusoe! Where were you? How did you get here?" Was I being rescued? Had someone finally come to get me? I opened one eye and saw Poll, perched on my chest. It was only the parrot!

"Oh Poll," I said as I rolled over and went back to sleep, "it's good to be home."

The feeling of being lost at sea stayed with me for the next few days. I was so scared. I could have lost everything. *No,* I thought, *no more sailing. It's not worth the risk.*

CHAPTER 21

The First Decade

Ten years passed. The gunpowder was running out. I needed to find a way to eat that didn't involve hunting. If I could catch a few young goat kids, I could tame them. If I could tame them, I would always have food—they would soon grow into a whole flock of goats.

It took me a few tries before I could capture the goats. The corn I set out would be eaten, but there would be no goat in the trap! The trap would be tripped, but there would be no animals in sight!

After three days of trying, I came back to the pit one morning to find goats munching away happily on the food that I had left. I led the goats to the meadow close to my summer home. There was already a nice hedge around the plot. I had set that up so the goats wouldn't escape once I got them to the grass. The three kids didn't like being tied up very much, but there was no other way to make sure they stayed put. I fed them corn and rice, and they liked it very much. They often ate it right out of my hands.

We carried on like this for a while. They ate what I gave them, and I kept them tied up. When I knew they wouldn't run wild anymore, I let them roam free over the meadow. The flock grew steadily over the next few years. So now, I had my harvest, my fruit trees, and my goats.

I was very proud of my growing farm. The corn grew well. The rice did, too. The flock gave me both meat and milk. All in all, things evolved as they should. I made more clothes from goatskin. Poll kept me in good company. Shippy grew old and died, though. And even though I thought about it all the time, I never did get back in that boat. Many, many years passed before I even went near where it was tied up!

You can only imagine what I looked like after spending ten whole years as a castaway! I wore goatskin clothes and a big, floppy hat. I had long hair and a long beard. My skin was often red and burnt. I didn't know anything about what was fashionable back home, and I guess it didn't really matter. There was no one on the island to see me anyway!

CHAPTER 22

The Footprint

One day, during my usual long morning walk, I decided to pick some grapes for raisins. But then, I had a flash of courage.

Maybe I'll go make sure my boat is still there, I thought. *I'm feeling brave today.* So, instead of visiting my summer house, I walked around to the beach where the boat was tied up. When I got there, I found a man's footprint in the sand.

"Oh no!" I exclaimed, "Who could that be? It must be the natives! I don't want them to see me! I don't want them to discover me!" I ran as fast as

I could all the way back to camp. I checked over my shoulder again and again as I ran. What if they found me? What would they do to me? After running for almost an hour, I made it back to my fence, jumped up onto my ladder, and pulled it in after me.

I tossed and turned in my sleep all that night. There were so many things I just didn't know—was it just one man, or more than one? Would they come for me? If they discovered my boat, they would know I was here! My heart beat very fast. My hands were shaky. I was afraid that everything I had built was about to be destroyed.

Three whole days passed before I even left my camp. And even then, I didn't want to go, but I needed water and my goats needed to be milked. I took a hidden path all the way to my summer house. I couldn't see anything out of the ordinary, so I spent a couple of days there trying to calm down.

Robinson, I thought to myself, *maybe you are overreacting. Maybe that footprint in the sand belonged to me, and I just didn't notice that I made it.* I mustered up all of my courage and walked back to the beach to take another look. The print was still there!

When I put my foot next to it, the print was almost twice as big! "It can't be!" I said. I started to shake and sweat all at once. It took me a couple of minutes to gather my thoughts, and then I raced home as fast as I could.

I spent another sleepless night thinking about that footprint. In a fit of craziness, I decided to rip all my crops and set my goats free—that way no one would know I was here. Morning dawned. The day was clear and bright. My farm was all still there. I knew then that I didn't need to destroy everything I had built. I just needed to be careful.

Two years passed and I didn't see a soul. No more footprints showed up on the sand. No one came and surprised me in the night. Life carried on as usual.

CHAPTER 23

No Smoke, No Fire

Years and years passed, and nothing much changed on my island. The rains came and went. The sun shone. My days continued as they had for many, many months. I came to love my early morning walks. Nothing made me happier than to make my way to my summer house, to see my goats, to look at my crops.

Then, as quickly as the rains could come, everything changed in an instant. I was walking to the other side of the island one morning when I saw them—the natives! There were great numbers of their canoes on shore. They were busy building a giant fire. I hid and watched them, wondering what to do. Instead of fleeing back to camp, I sat down and thought about it logically.

I have been here for almost twenty years, and they have never found me. They have never even seen me. If I stay hidden, they might never find me.

I slipped away from the shore and went home. I wanted to get on with my life, but I knew things would never be the same.

My morning ritual from that day forward included safety measures. I would hike up to the top of the lookout hill with my old binoculars and take a look around. Instead of watching for ships, I looked out for the canoes. Weeks, then months, went by. I came to the conclusion that my island must not be a spot they visited often. Maybe years would pass again before they came back. Maybe they would never come back.

The most important thing on my mind was making my life on the island as invisible as possible. The biggest problem I had to solve was how to make a fire without smoke. I didn't want to start a fire in my cold storage cave; that would smoke out my entire camp. No, I needed to find a cave away from my camp. The smoke was really the only evidence that another human being was living on the island. Without the smoke, the natives might never discover my camp or my summer home.

It took me a couple of days before I found a place that would work. The cave was quite big. As I walked deeper inside, I found that I could easily stand up in the middle of it.

Then, something happened that scared me to my bare bones! While exploring the cave, I turned a corner and came face-to-face with a pair of bright eyes staring right back at me. What a shock! After getting my breath back, I took a closer look.

There was a sick, old billy goat just lying there. He didn't want to move and I didn't make him. I just gave him a sip of my water and left him alone.

The next day I came back to the cave with some supplies. I had some candles and some other things. The cave had a long narrow hallway that led to a beautiful room. It sparkled in the light with bright, twinkling lights.

Maybe it's diamonds! I thought. But now was not the time to think about mining!

The cave was safe and dry so I decided to store the rest of my gunpowder there, along with my extra guns. I also did most of my cooking inside, where no one could see the smoke from my fire.

CHAPTER 24

Another Shipwreck?

Now, my homes on the island were secure. My cooking cave worked well, and my daily watches were a good routine. I felt safe, but I still kept busy to keep my mind off the natives.

One awful night, I heard a cannon shot in the distance. I raced up to my lookout hill and tried to see what might be out there—but it was too dark.

"It must be a ship in distress!" I said to the night. "They could rescue me!"

Even though I knew it was dangerous, I lit a big bonfire.

"They must see it! They must!" I muttered to myself as I scrambled to keep the fire blazing. The winds were high and it was a challenge to keep it all under control. Almost moments later, I heard two more cannon shots, and then a few gun shots. They must have seen my signal!

Dawn soon arrived. The fog started to clear up as the sun warmed the island. I could just barely make out a ship in the distance. I ran all the way to the south side of the island. I dropped to my knees as soon as I reached the beach. A wreck! Oh no! Those poor men—their ship was dashed on the very rocks that almost killed me all those years ago. My heart sank as I knew there could be no survivors. They sent out a signal and no ship saved them. In the dark, they must not have seen my island.

I wept. "If only one had survived, just one!" I felt more alone at that very moment than I had in all of the twenty-odd years I had spent by myself.

The only choice I had to make now was whether or not to use my boat and see if I could gather supplies. In the end, I decided it was worth the risk. But I waited until the next morning, when the tide was low. I didn't want to get swept out to sea.

As soon as I came close to the boat, I heard a dog barking. I called out to him and he jumped right in my boat. He was a scrappy little fellow, that's for sure. Much of the ship's cargo was ruined by the water. But I managed to save a few copper pots, a few seamen's chests, some barrels of liquid, and some gunpowder. The ship was very unstable. I worked quickly and packed everything up on my little boat.

It took me lots of trips to carry the cargo back to my camp. What riches I found when I finally opened up the chests. They were full of extraordinary treasures! One had a fine case of bottles, filled with flavored drinks. They were delicious, that's for sure. Another was filled with sweetmeats, and yet another carried brand-new shirts. In the last chest I opened, there were three great big bags of gold. They just sat there next to two pairs of shoes! I stored a lot of these new-found treasures in my cave, just to make sure they were safe.

The excitement of my discoveries barely lasted two or three days. I ate up all the sweetmeats and drank all the cordial waters. Life returned to normal. It was back to checking the lookout every morning. But something was different now because I had a new dog to keep me company. I named him Scruffy. He was an excellent little companion.

Soon after the shipwreck, I celebrated my twenty-fourth year on the island. Hours passed that day as I sat and thought about everything that had happened. They were happy years of hard work and lots of success. But now, I spent so much time worrying about being discovered by the natives that it was hard to enjoy my life. My anniversary passed and I convinced myself it was time to escape. But how would I get off the island?

I spent the entire rainy season that year thinking and planning an escape. The key to all of my plans were the natives. If I could make peace with them, they would be able to show me a way off the island.

Would it work? Would I be able to make friends with them?

CHAPTER 25

Robinson Meets Friday

Many months passed before fate answered my questions. I had not been out long one morning before I discovered the canoes. The natives were back! They were camping in the same place as they had done a couple of years ago. Again, I hid and watched them from a distance.

They had two prisoners with them. These poor men were tied up with vine ropes and looked scared to death. I knew then there was no hope of making friends with these scary men.

There were at least thirty of them! They were making a lot of strange noises. One very large man knocked down one of the prisoners with his bare hands. After watching his companion get hit, the second man took the chance of his life and sped away. He ran faster than any man I had ever seen run before! Before I knew what was happening, he turned and ran toward me.

My heart almost stopped still in my chest. *This is it,* I imagined, *they're going to find me now, and then they're going to hurt me.*

Two other men chased the prisoner. They all came closer and closer to me. In a split second, I made up my mind to help the poor man. I crouched in the bushes and waited until just the right moment. The prisoner ran by me. Then, I stepped out and tripped one of the men chasing him. The second man tried to grab me, but I managed to knock him out cold. The prisoner turned around and saw me there.

"Don't worry!" I said, knowing he probably didn't understand me, "I'm going to help you!"

The man hesitated for a minute, and then he ran back to me. "Help me tie them up, so they can't hurt you anymore." At first he didn't understand, but then I cut his wrists free of the vines and pointed to the two men. We tied them up using the same kind of vine ropes. They would not be moving for a very long time!

"Come on!" I said. "We need to get out of here."

I brought the man to my cave. When we could finally rest, I gave him some food and water—he was very hungry and thirsty.

"What's your name?" I asked.

He answered me in his language.

"I'm going to call you Friday," I said. "Because that's the day I rescued you!"

The man smiled at me and nodded. I pointed

at my chest, "My name is Robinson. Robinson Crusoe."

Before he could help himself, Friday let out a great, big yawn. I laughed out loud. "You must be very tired." I showed him the straw sleeping mat I kept in the cave and said, "Here, why don't you take a nap."

Friday smiled at me. He knew exactly what I meant. He walked over to the mat and fell right asleep. I just sat there and watched him for a while. Even though I knew he didn't understand me and I didn't understand him, it was wonderful to have someone to talk to. Friday was a very tall man. He had long, dark hair that fell right down his back. He was dressed in skins as well, but didn't wear quite as many as I did.

The next day, I came back to my cooking cave to find Friday still there. In fact, over the next few days, I was very surprised to find that he didn't want to go home at all. For more than two months we worked hard side-by-side. We got along well, even if we didn't speak the same language.

CHAPTER 26

Life with a Friend

Friday and I spent the next three years living and working together. We fell into a very comfortable routine. In the mornings we would check the island to make sure the natives hadn't returned. In the afternoons, we would work on the farm, tend to the crops, milk the goats, or pick fruit. In the evenings, we would make our dinner and I would teach Friday my language. I trusted him completely.

Fortune had answered my prayers. I was no longer alone. Just having Friday around made me less afraid of being discovered. I knew that the two of us together had a better chance of protecting ourselves against the natives. It also made me think more and more about escaping. I asked Friday many questions during this time. Where were we? Who were his people? What islands were nearby? Did he miss his family? Would his family be looking for him?

For the most part, he smiled and nodded a reply, until he learned my language and could answer me.

"Friday," I asked, "how come you don't want to go home to your island?"

"A long time ago, I left home. I wanted to see the world. My father was very angry with me. He did not want me to go. I was on my way to have a great voyage when I was caught by the natives. Then, you saved my life."

"Do you miss your father?"

Friday thought for a minute. "I do miss him. I

miss my island. But I like it here. I like living here, working on the farm. It's very different."

I smiled. "So you want to stay?"

Friday grinned from ear to ear. "Of course I do! It's a chance of a lifetime to have such an adventure!"

"We're a lot alike, you and I," I said. "That's how I ended up on the island, too. I left home for a great adventure—and landed here over twenty years ago."

I spent hours telling Friday about my life before the island, about growing up in England, about my plantation in Brazil. He told me about his life, about his family, and about what it was like living on the island where he came from. We had so much in common, despite being born in very different places. We became the best of friends.

"We were meant to be great friends, Robinson! I'm not worried. I know everything will be okay."

We sat quietly in our tent for a while after that, each of us thinking about how he ended up here, each of us lost in his own thoughts about the life of an adventurer.

"Friday," I asked, "do any of your people ever get swept out to sea in their boats?"

"No," he replied. "I don't think so. We row with the tide. It works well. The river runs through it all."

At first, I didn't understand what he meant. What river? Of course! I realized he must mean the great Orinoco River. My island must be near Trinidad.

"Have you seen many men like me before?" I pointed to my beard.

Friday thought about this for a minute. Then he answered, "A great way beyond the moon. Far away from my people, far away from here, there are whiskered men. Men with long beards and pale faces, just like you, yes."

Friday's words made me very excited. "Do you think we could we sail there from here in my small boat?"

He shook his head. My spirits fell. "Not in the small boat, no. But we could sail in a bigger boat—big, like two canoes."

I grinned from ear to ear. I slapped Friday on the back out of happiness. He looked at me like I was crazy, but I didn't care. For the first time in over twenty years, I had an idea of where I had landed. I had an idea of where my island was in relation to the world. I wasn't alone, and I had a hope of going home.

One lazy afternoon during the dry season, Friday and I took a long walk down to the beach where I had seen the footprint. I wanted to show him the pieces of the old ship that I had taken apart and hidden all those years ago.

Friday studied the wreckage of the boat for a long time. He turned the pieces over to look underneath. He walked all the way around it more than once. Then, he put his hand on his chin and said, "I've seen a boat like this before, Robinson."

I was very surprised to hear that. "What do you mean?" I asked.

Friday looked at me and replied, "Four years ago. Yes, it was four years ago and seventeen men landed at my nation." He continued on to tell me that these men were still there, living on his island, near his people.

"They must be men from the shipwreck I saw!" I told Friday all about how I had heard cannon shots that night, and then gunfire. "But when the fog cleared and I came down to the beach, all I could find was another broken ship! How wonderful that all those men didn't die that night as I thought they did!"

We started to walk back to camp, both of us

lost in our own thoughts. It was a quiet walk, and I didn't say anything to my friend until after dinner.

"Friday," I said decidedly, "we must go back to your island!"

CHAPTER 27

Can We Get off the Island?

We needed a boat if we were going to escape. The two that I had built (for my first boat still lay marooned on land in the middle of the forest) would not work for such a long journey.

"Friday, do you think you can help me build a boat like the one you saw four years ago?" I asked him one morning over breakfast.

"Yes, I don't see why not." He answered. "I'm not sure I know how, but I'm sure you can teach me—right, Robinson?"

"Of course!" I said. "With both of us working

on it, we should be able to build a nice boat to take us back to your island."

We chopped down trees. We carved out planks. We hollowed out the bottom. We worked and worked. Months passed while our boat slowly took shape. We worked all the way through an entire dry season without stopping for even one day. Once the boat was finished, it took all of our energy to inch it bit-by-bit into the water. You had never seen two happier men the day the boat floated in the water for the first time!

Friday was confident we could use our paddles and row all the way to the mainland. I had a better idea, though. While Friday chopped down a large cedar tree to use as a mast, I sat and sewed together all the bits of canvas I had been saving over the years. We put the mast in and set the sail up. The boat was now ready for a trial run! Friday and I boated around the harbor as I taught him how to sail. Like everything else I had shown him how to do, he was a quick learner. Soon, Friday knew how to handle the boat almost as well as I did!

We then had to retire indoors for a rainy season. The boat needed to be protected from the weather. We dug a small dock out of the earth near the creek. Then, we kept it dry by building a dam up around it and piling large, full branches on top to make a roof. Now, all there was left to do was wait for better weather.

A total of twenty-seven years had passed since I was shipwrecked on the island. It was hard to believe that so much time had gone by.

I would sit for long periods of time and wonder how much life had changed back home. Was my plantation still there? Was my family still alive? Did my brother ever come home? These thoughts ran through my head like raindrops, and nothing but the sunshine could stop them.

CHAPTER 28

Mutiny and Freedom

The rains stopped, just as they had done for many seasons. Friday and I started to prepare in earnest for our trip. We took good care with the harvest, and started organizing all of our supplies. The only thing left to do was make sure we had enough food.

"Friday?" I asked. "Would you mind hiking down to the summer house and gathering up some raisins for us?"

"Not at all," he replied. "I'll go right now."

An hour had barely passed when I heard him

running up the path screaming, "Robinson! Robinson, come quickly. There's a boat out here! A boat!"

I grabbed two guns on my way out the door and tossed one to Friday. We sped off to the look-out hill. We both hid quietly and watched as an English ship sailed toward the island.

"What do you think they are doing?" Friday whispered.

"I don't know," I replied. "But it can't be anything good. This isn't a regular trade route—I haven't seen an English ship in almost thirty years."

The ship set down its anchor just off the beach. A group of rough, angry men dragged three prisoners off the boat and on to the shore. They had both their hands and feet bound. Then, the wicked men left these poor fellows in the hot sun with no food or water as they went off to explore the island.

I motioned for Friday to follow me. We crept

slowly down the path to the beach. When I was sure there was no one around, I snuck up to the men and asked them who they were and why they had come to the island.

They were very confused at first and didn't answer me at all. I must have looked like quite a sight to them—a wild and crazy man appearing out of nowhere!

"I won't hurt you," I said. "I'm here to help." I called for Friday to come out and he cut their binds with his knife. As they were being freed, one of the men explained, "I am the captain of this great ship. There was a mutiny on board. The crew decided to sail off course and that's how we landed here."

"Come quickly," I said to them. "We need to get you three out of here before they get back."

"I'm Captain Walsh, by the way. These two men are my first-mates, Morgan and Pace."

"I'm Robinson Crusoe, and this is Friday."

CHAPTER 29

Taking Charge

With the introductions out of the way, we ran as fast as we could off the beach, with Friday leading the way. Once we were sitting safely on the lookout hill, the captain told us his story in greater detail. In the end, it was just two men causing all the problems for the poor captain. They had convinced the others to mutiny and were now leading them all astray. It was lucky they even survived, the captain said, for the two were terrible sailors—they didn't really know what they were doing at all.

"Gold is the only thing they think about—not about the safety of the boat, or of the lives of the rest of the men. Money is the only thing they want."

I asked Captain Walsh if he thought the rest of his men would return to loyalty if the two bandits were caught.

"Yes. I think they would. I don't think they're too happy to be at sea with no clear direction and no plans to go home."

I told Captain Walsh that Friday and I would be happy to help him, but I needed to know two things first.

"Will you follow my instructions and let me lead you in this fight? And should we win, will you take Friday and me back to England with you?"

Captain Walsh agreed immediately. The five of us sat for a long while and created a very good plan. The two villains often spent time just sitting and hatching their plans. The captain agreed we could probably capture them easily, and then when they were safely tied up, convince the rest of the men to return to order.

We took the sailors to my cooking cave, where the rest of my guns were stored. I gave each man a weapon and some gunpowder, just in case we needed it. We five moved as soft as air back down to the beach. The men were all taking a nap, spread out all over the beach, some with their heads on logs, some just laying in the sun.

We surrounded the men, and I counted to three with my fingers. We all fired our guns into the air at the same time. The men jumped up, scared and shocked. They didn't know what to do!

"Toss your weapons!" I yelled. "Do it now before we shoot you all!"

The clank and crash of many knives, swords, and scabbards rang out as they hit the ground.

"Guns, too—I know you have some!" A few men reluctantly parted with their weapons.

I turned to the captain, "Who are the villains who took over your ship, Captain Walsh?" The captain pointed his finger at two men cowering in the middle of the group.

"You two—come here, now!" They hesitated at first, and then they tried to make a run for it. But Friday was too quick for them. He tripped the first one and then grabbed the other before he could even make it to the trees.

"Quick!" I said. "Let's get them tied up!" Morgan and Pace tied their hands together with some vines.

"Friday, you know where to take these two ruffians!" He nodded and motioned for Pace and Morgan to help him.

Once they were out of earshot, the captain spoke to his men. He told them they could either come back to him or lose their lives today—it was their choice. They all hung their heads in shame for betraying such a good man. Every single one

of them told Captain Walsh that they would follow him. Many apologized for the mutiny, and said they were deeply upset about they way they acted. Someone even started up a chorus of "For He's a Jolly Good Fellow," which made Captain Walsh very happy.

With the two villains were safely tied up in my cooking cave, the captain and I had a chance to have a nice, long talk. I gave Captain Walsh a tour of my island, and showed him our successful farm. He was very impressed. He couldn't believe that I had done so much all by myself!

After a lifetime on the island, it only took Friday and me a couple of hours to pack everything we needed for the voyage to England. The captain said he had plenty of supplies on board already, but took some drinking water and a lot of the fruit from my summer house for the trip back. And then the kind captain gave me a clean shirt and a new pair of pants! They were marvelous—it had been years since I had worn anything other than goatskin clothes!

"Friday," I asked when we were packing, "Are you sure you don't want to return home to your family?"

"Robinson," he answered, "I decided a long, long time ago that I wanted a life of adventure. Now, I've got the chance to see the great nation of England, and I'm not about to pass that up!"

"Oh, Friday!" I said. "I'm so happy to hear you're coming along with me. It just wouldn't be the same without you."

Captain Walsh came to tell us that his ship was ready to go. There was just one more thing I needed to do before we left—I visited the two men tied up in my cooking cave.

"You have two choices," I said. "You can return to England with us—bound and shackled—destined to be tried and hung for treason. Or, you can stay here, on this island, and do your best to survive."

The two men looked at each other. They knew that to return to the mainland would mean execution. So I wasn't surprised when both men hung their heads and accepted their fate. I untied their hands and feet and left them some drinking water. I told them where they could find my camp, and how to live well on the island if they worked hard. They didn't look very happy when I left, but at least they were alive.

"This island is a paradise now, and you must treat it as such."

With those parting words, I left them. I took one last look around. The day I thought would never come was finally here—I was getting off the island. My prison had become a beautiful home. But as comfortable as it had all become, I longed for civilization. I wanted to go home.

CHAPTER 30

Home Again

I met Friday in front of the summer house and we walked down to the beach together. I had already packed the few things I wanted to take with me: my goatskin hat, my umbrella, and my latest pet parrot. Of course, all of the money I had found and saved all those years ago would now come in very handy!

We left the island on December 19, 1686—twenty-eight years, two months, and nineteen days after I had landed there. By June of the next year, we had made our way back to England. As I walked through the streets of York, I couldn't believe how much had changed in the last thirty-five years. The town was bigger. The streets were busier. My mother and father had both passed away years ago. In my heart I didn't really expect them to be alive, but I was sad over the loss anyway.

After spending some time in York, I decided to travel to Brazil. I was curious to see what had happened to my plantation—to see if my partners were still alive and if my farm still existed.

Friday and I set off by sea to Brazil. It was now April 1688. The country had changed so much! Many of my friends and old business partners had passed away. Luckily, Wells, my old friend and neighbor, was still alive. He had grown very rich from the success of both of our plantations. When Friday and I arrived on his doorstep, he was so surprised to see me—at first, he didn't even recognize me! My plantation was restored to me, and I made a very good profit when I sold it a couple of months later.

The plans to return to England were soon set in motion. I longed for a peaceful, quiet life, the very same kind of life my father wanted for me all those years ago. Long before I set off on any adventure. Long before I spent almost all of my life stranded on a deserted island. Perhaps now, in my golden years, I could truly enjoy the life he wanted for me. But Friday and I would have to get home first, and those adventures, my faithful friends, are the tales of another story.

What Do *You* Think?

Questions for Discussion

Have you ever been around a toddler who keeps asking the question "Why?" Does your teacher call on you in class with questions from your homework? Do your parents ask you questions about your day at the dinner table? We are always surrounded by questions that need a specific response. But is it possible to have a question with no right answer?

The following questions are about the book you just read. But this is not a quiz! They are designed to help you look at the people, places, and events in the story from different angles. These questions do not have specific answers. Instead, they might make you think of the story in a completely new way.

Think carefully about each question and enjoy discovering more about this classic story.

1. At the beginning of the book, Robinson claims that he "craved grand adventures and far-away lands." Do you think he still feels this way at the end of the book? What place would you like to visit most?

2. Robinson's parents try everything they can to make him change his mind about being a sailor. Do you think they're right to do so? Has anyone ever tried to make you change your mind about something? Did it work?

3. Robinson quickly finds out that life at sea is not what he expected. Have you ever dreamed about something only to find out that the reality is very different?

4. Robinson never seems to stay in one place for long. In Brazil, he sets up a farm and is beginning to settle down, but his desire for excitement and travel gets the best of him. Would you leave the safety of your home to go exploring?

5. When Robinson arrives on the island, he quickly discovers that he is the only one of his shipmates to have survived. What would you have done in his place? Have you ever been completely alone?

6. After a few weeks on the island, Robinson begins to keep a diary. He says, "On the days where my heart ached with everything I had lost or given up, it helped to write." Do you keep a diary? When do you write in it?

7. Robinson says, "How glorious home is when you've been away." Do you agree with this statement? What was the longest time you were ever away from home?

8. One of Robinson's most frightening moments on the island occurs when he finds a footprint. How would you have reacted if you were in his position? What's the scariest thing that ever happened to you?

9. Robinson says that his one special talent is the ability to survive. Do you agree? What is your special talent?

10. What trait do you most admire in Robinson? What trait do you least like about him? Is there one thing in particular that you like or dislike about yourself?

Afterword

First impressions are important.

Whether we are meeting new people, going to new places, or picking up a book unknown to us, first impressions count for a lot. They can lead to warm, lasting memories or can make us shy away from any future encounters.

Can you recall your own first impressions and earliest memories of reading the classics?

Do you remember wading through pages and pages of text to prepare for an exam? Or were you the child who hid under the blanket to read with a flashlight, joining forces with Robin Hood to save Maid Marian? Do you remember only how long it took you to read a lengthy novel such as *Little Women*? Or did you become best friends with the March sisters?

Even for a gifted young reader, getting through long chapters with dense language can easily become overwhelming and can obscure the richness of the story and its characters. Reading an abridged, newly crafted version of a classic novel can be the gentle introduction a child needs to explore the characters and story line without the frustration of difficult vocabulary and complex themes.

Reading an abridged version of a classic novel gives the young reader a sense of independence and the satisfaction of finishing a "grown-up" book. And when a child is engaged with and inspired by a classic story, the tone is set for further exploration of the story's themes, characters, history, and details. As a child's reading skills advance, the desire to tackle the original, unabridged version of the story will naturally emerge.

If made accessible to young readers, these stories can become invaluable tools for understanding themselves in the context of their families and social environments. This is why the *Classic Starts* series includes questions that stimulate discussion regarding the impact and social relevance of the characters and stories today. These questions can foster lively conversations between children and their parents or teachers. When we look at the issues, values, and standards of past times in terms of how we live now, we can appreciate literature's classic tales in a very personal and engaging way.

Share your love of reading the classics with a young child, and introduce an imaginary world real enough to last a lifetime.

Dr. Arthur Pober, Ed.D.

Dr. Arthur Pober has spent more than twenty years in the fields of early-childhood and gifted education. He is the former principal of one of the world's oldest laboratory schools for gifted youngsters, Hunter College Elementary School, and former Director of Magnet Schools for the Gifted and Talented for more than 25,000 youngsters in New York City.

Dr. Pober is a recognized authority in the areas of media and child protection and is currently the U.S. representative to the European Institute for the Media and European Advertising Standards Alliance.

Explore these wonderful stories in our Classic Starts library.

20,000 Leagues Under the Sea

The Adventures of Huckleberry Finn

The Adventures of Robin Hood

The Adventures of Sherlock Holmes

The Adventures of Tom Sawyer

Anne of Green Gables

Black Beauty

Call of the Wild

Frankenstein

Gulliver's Travels

A Little Princess

Little Women

Oliver Twist

The Red Badge of Courage

Robinson Crusoe

The Secret Garden

The Story of King Arthur and His Knights

The Strange Case of Dr. Jekyll and Mr. Hyde

Treasure Island

White Fang